The Silver Charm

A FOLKTALE FROM JAPAN

BY ROBERT D. SAN SOUCI

ILLUSTRATED BY

YORIKO ITO

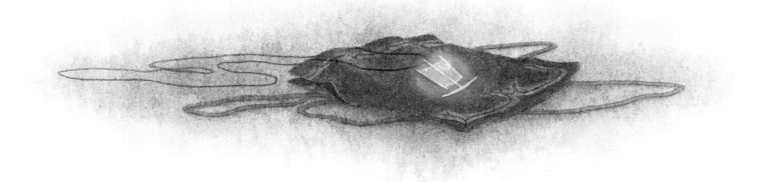

A DOUBLEDAY BOOK
FOR YOUNG READERS

CHILDREN'S ROOM

For Robert Kikuchi-Yngojo and Nancy Wang and Eth-Noh-Tec—ROBERT D. SAN SOUCI

For my beloved cat, Michael, my best friend for fourteen years—YORIKO ITO

Sources

Primary sources for this adaptation include Basil Hall Chamberlain, *Aino Folk-Tales** (originally printed by the American Folk-Lore Society in 1888; reprinted by Nendeln/Liechtenstein, Germany: Kraus Reprints Limited, 1967), and Violet Moore Higgins, *The Silver Ship: And Other Japanese Tales Retold* (Racine/Chicago: Whitman Publishing Company, 1917).

Among numerous volumes of background material that I consulted, I found the most helpful to be A. H. Savage Landor, *Alone with the Hairy Ainu; or, 3,800 Miles on a Pack Saddle in Yezo and a Cruise to the Kurile Islands* (London: John Murray, 1893); John Batchelor, "Items of Ainu Folk-Lore," *Journal of American Folk-Lore* 7 (1894): 15–44; M. Inez Hilger, *Together with the Ainu: A Vanishing People* (Norman: University of Oklahoma Press, 1971); the series of articles on aspects of Ainu culture by John Batchelor, issued from 1882 through 1888 in *Transactions of the Asiatic Society of Japan*, obtained from the San Francisco Public Library; and "Brochure on the Ainu People," published by the Ainu Association of Hokkaido.

* In the 1800s, *Aino* was a widely used variant of *Ainu*. The word *Ainu* means "human" in the Ainu language. The word can also mean "man" or "husband."

A Doubleday Book for Young Readers
Published by Random House Children's Books
a division of Random House, Inc.
1540 Broadway, New York, New York 10036
Doubleday and the anchor with dolphin colophon are registered trademarks of Random House, Inc.

Text copyright © 2002 by Robert D. San Souci
Illustrations copyright © 2002 by Yoriko Ito

Visit us on the Web! www.randomhouse.com/kids
Educators and librarians, for a variety of teaching tools, visit us at
www.randomhouse.com/teachers

Library of Congress Cataloging-in-Publication Data
San Souci, Robert D.
    The silver charm / by Robert D. San Souci ; illustrated by Yoriko Ito.
        p.   cm.
    Summary: In this folktale from Japan's Ainu people, a pet puppy and fox retrieve their young master's good luck charm from the ogre who has stolen it.
    ISBN 0-385-32159-7 (trade)   0-385-90847-4 (lib. bdg.)
    [1. Ainu—Folklore. 2. Folklore—Japan.] I. Ito, Yoriko, ill. II. Title.
    PZ8.1.S227Sk 1999
    398.2089946—dc21   97-44157

The text of this book is set in 16-point Weiss. • Book design by Trish Parcell Watts
Manufactured in the United States of America • May 2002
10 9 8 7 6 5 4 3 2 1

Author's Note

This folktale comes from Japan's Ainu (*eye-noo*), an indigenous people who live on the island of Hokkaido (formerly Yezo), the Kurile Islands, and southern Sakhalin. The Ainu have distinct physical characteristics, their own language, and unique social, cultural, and religious traditions. Though Ainu culture was established by the twelfth century, the people's origins remain uncertain to this day.   —*Robert D. San Souci*

Artist's Note

While doing research for this book, I was drawn to the beauty of Ainu culture, which is filled with gods (*Kamui*) and legends (*Kamui yukara*).

I visited an Ainu Village (*Ainu kotan*), Nibutani village in Hokkaido, which, Kamui yukara state, is the source of Ainu culture. While there, I stayed with an Ainu family who provided me with helpful information and advice.

Special thanks to Mr. Matsuyama and Mr. and Mrs. Kaizuka for their invaluable help in my research.

—*Yoriko Ito*

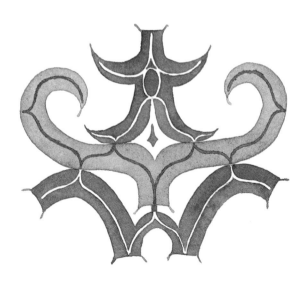

In the north of Japan is the island called Hokkaido, where the Ainu people live. Long ago, a fisherman and his wife lived in a small seaside village. They had one son, Satsu. For company, Satsu kept a puppy and a fox cub, whom he loved dearly and cared for tenderly. The puppy and fox cub went everywhere Satsu went.

Satsu's parents gave him his way in almost everything, but they insisted on two rules:

"Do not go near the woods," his mother warned. "The ogre there catches and eats disobedient children."

"Take care not to lose your good-luck charm," said his father. "It belonged to my father and his father before him. It has always brought good fortune to the sons in my family."

The charm was a tiny silver ship, with masts no thicker than a bamboo sliver and sails as thin as rice paper. To keep it safe, his mother sewed a little charm bag and hung it on a cord around Satsu's neck.

"If you lose this," she cautioned, "misfortune is sure to follow."

Satsu promised to obey and to be careful.

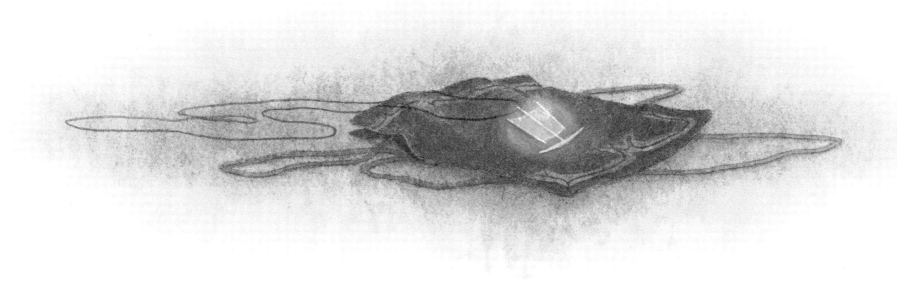

One day Satsu went to the beach with his fox and pup. For a time, he watched men gather *kombu*, brown seaweed, while women set it on rocks to dry. He took out his silver ship and pretended to sail it across the waves, singing,

Ankaya chippo hoochip.
Soriri katta chopnit.

Let us ride on a boat.
Let us sail on the ocean.

Then he put it back and went exploring, gathering shells and pretty stones, while the puppy and the fox raced up and down the shore, chasing each other. Splashing in and out of the waves, they forgot their little master for a time.

Suddenly the fox cub cried, "Oh, where is Satsu?"
"We must find him!" said the puppy. "We are near
the ogre's forest, and I am afraid for our master."

Indeed, Satsu had wandered to the edge of the woods. Just within the forest, he saw tangled raspberry and blackberry vines. Satsu was so hungry and the scent of the ripe berries was so sweet that he forgot his mother's warning. He went into the woods and happily began picking and eating the berries.

With a roar, a hideous ogre suddenly burst from the shadow of the trees. As tall as two men, the monster had hairy skin, a mouth filled with fearsome teeth, blazing red eyes, and two white horns. Satsu turned to run, but his robe caught on the thorns of the berry vines. Then the ogre stretched out his long arm and snatched up the boy in his big clawed hand.

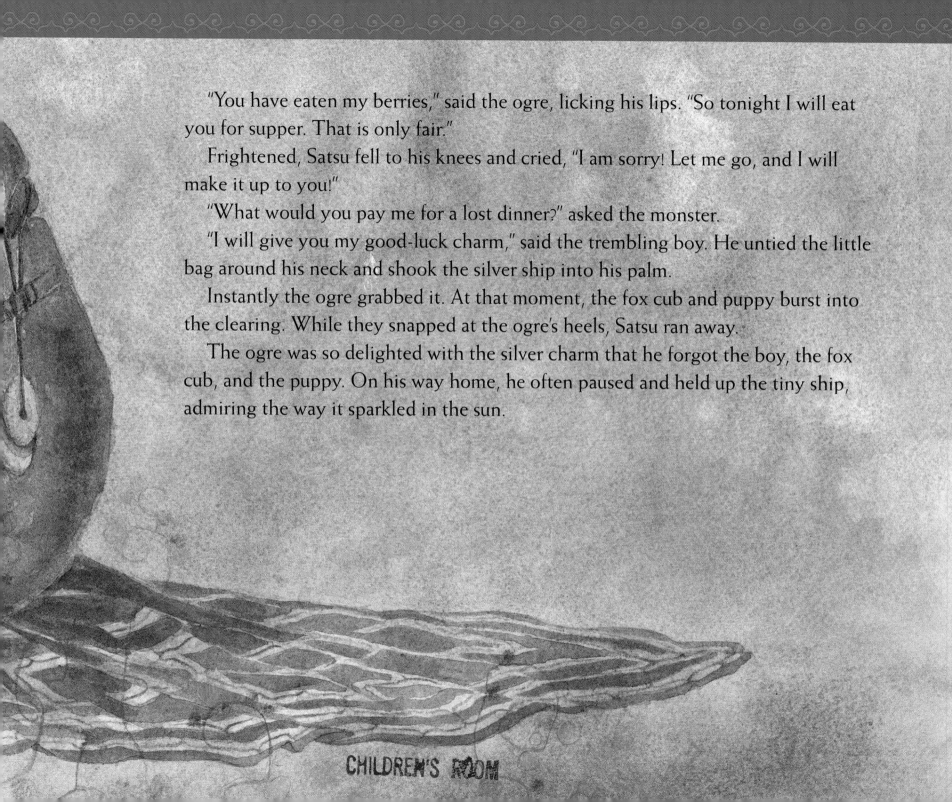

"You have eaten my berries," said the ogre, licking his lips. "So tonight I will eat you for supper. That is only fair."

Frightened, Satsu fell to his knees and cried, "I am sorry! Let me go, and I will make it up to you!"

"What would you pay me for a lost dinner?" asked the monster.

"I will give you my good-luck charm," said the trembling boy. He untied the little bag around his neck and shook the silver ship into his palm.

Instantly the ogre grabbed it. At that moment, the fox cub and puppy burst into the clearing. While they snapped at the ogre's heels, Satsu ran away.

The ogre was so delighted with the silver charm that he forgot the boy, the fox cub, and the puppy. On his way home, he often paused and held up the tiny ship, admiring the way it sparkled in the sun.

The moment Satsu left the woods, his stomach began to ache and his head to burn, because he had eaten the ogre's berries. He felt weak and lay down. While the fox guarded his master, the puppy hurried home. He barked and barked until Satsu's worried parents followed him back to the feverish boy.

Satsu's father carried him home, while his anxious mother and pets followed. His mother put him to bed. When she discovered that the little bag around his neck was empty, she cried, "He has lost his good-luck charm!"

Then Satsu's father said, "Surely this is what has brought him such misfortune."

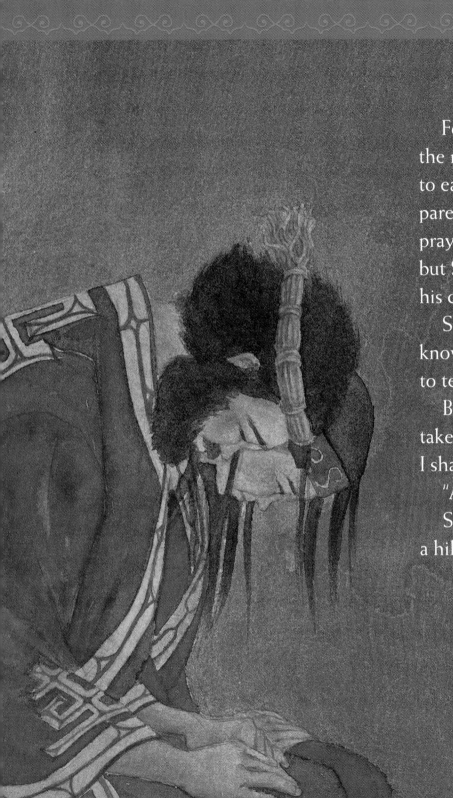

Fox and puppy watched over their master through the night. The next morning, Satsu was too ill even to eat the millet soup his mother cooked. His parents sent for the village shaman. The wise man prayed to the *kamui*, spirits, to cool the boy's fever; but Satsu grew worse. Then the healer said, "Unless his charm is returned, the boy will surely die."

Satsu's mother and father despaired. They did not know where the charm was, and Satsu was too sick to tell.

But the fox cub said to the puppy, "Let us go and take the charm back from the ogre. For if Satsu dies, I shall die of a broken heart."

"And so shall I," the puppy agreed.

So they set out for the ogre's *chise*, his hut, high on a hill above the forest.

As they trotted through the thick woods, the fox said, "I am hungry."

And the puppy said, "We were foolish not to bring some dried fish or a bone for our journey."

Just then, they spotted a plump mouse. They gave chase and trapped the mouse between them. Before they could gobble him up, however, the mouse bowed, touching his head to the ground.

"Lord Fox! Lord Hound! Please be merciful," the wretched creature begged. "Do not eat me! I have a wife and ten small mouslings at home."

Hearing this, the tenderhearted puppy said, "Go back to your family."

"We will not harm you," agreed the fox.

But the grateful mouse said, "Let me do something to help you in return."

"We are on a mission of great importance," said the fox. "There is nothing you could do to help us."

"Nevertheless," said the mouse, "there is a saying that the merciful find help in unexpected places. Tell me where you are going."

Quickly the puppy told of the stolen charm and Satsu's illness. "Now we are going to the ogre's hut. But how we will recover the silver ship, I cannot guess."

"Perhaps I *can* help!" said the mouse. "Not long ago, I visited the shaman's house. As I dined upon his rice, I heard him tell a visitor some secret words that will turn one thing into another. Maybe this will help you."

The mouse told the fox cub and puppy to gather leaves and glue them together with sap. When they had dressed up in their leafy outfits, he gave the puppy a strip of elm bark and the fox a stick.

Finally the mouse was ready. As he spoke the magic words, the fox cub turned into a dancing boy in bright silk garments, and the puppy became a dancing girl in a beautiful kimono. The elm bark became a cloth the girl threw over her shoulders; the stick became a sword in the boy's hands. The mouse hid in the girl's kimono.

"While you dance for the ogre," said the mouse, "I will secretly look for the silver charm. When I find it, I will turn you back into your proper shapes. Then we must all run for our lives and for the life of your master!"

Off they went in their disguises. When they reached the ogre's hut, the boy cleared his throat to announce their arrival.

The monster lifted the mat that guarded the entrance and glared at them. The boy and the girl and the hidden mouse saw the silver charm on a cord around his neck.

"*Nishpa*, sir," said the boy and girl together, kneeling and bowing their heads, "we are lost. If we dance for you, will you give us food and show us the way out of these woods?"

"Perhaps," said the ogre with a sly grin, "if you amuse me." In fact, he planned to watch, then make them his dinner.

The ogre invited the boy and girl inside. A fire burned in a pit at the center of the hut, filling it with smoke.

"Dance!" commanded the ogre, sitting beside a lacquer box filled with *sake*, rice wine. He dipped up a bowlful and drank noisily.

The mouse crept out of the girl's kimono and carefully climbed up the back of the ogre's robe. He began to chew on the cord that held Satsu's good-luck charm.

To distract the ogre, the girl danced the Crane Dance while the boy clapped his hands and kept time. She pretended to be a crane, moving the sleeves of her kimono up and down as though she were flapping her wings. Then she circled and gently dropped to her knees, folding her head under her cloth like a bird coming to rest.

"*Pirika!*" cried the ogre. "Very pretty!"

Meanwhile the mouse nibbled, nibbled, nibbled.

Then the boy began the Sword Dance. While the girl clapped, he danced, stamping his feet loudly. All the time, he kept his eyes on the mouse, half hidden in the folds of the ogre's robe.

How the monster laughed to see the boy dance!

When the boy saw that the mouse had nearly bitten through the cord, he nodded to the girl. She stood up and began to dance alongside him, clapping ever more quickly. The ogre dropped his *sake* bowl and clapped too.

Suddenly the boy stamped his feet fiercely and lunged forward. The startled ogre tumbled over backward to escape the sword point. At that instant, the mouse bit through the last strand and leapt away with the charm in his mouth.

Bellowing, the ogre clambered to his feet. But the mouse squeaked a magic word, and boy and girl became fox cub and puppy once again. They scurried as fast as they could out the door.

The ogre lumbered after them, but they ran into the brush. They could hear the monster snapping off branches and ripping up vines behind them. Still they ran and ran, following the hidden paths that only the smallest creatures know, and soon they left the ogre far behind.

At the edge of the forest, the mouse gave the little fox and puppy the charm.

"Thank you! Thank you!" Satsu's pets said, bowing.

Bowing in return, the mouse said, "I am glad I was able to repay you for the kindness you showed me." Then he scampered off to his mouse hole and his waiting family. The puppy held the charm gently in his mouth while the fox cub kept watch for the ogre. Soon they reached Satsu's home. There they placed the charm beside their sleeping master's head.

Gently the puppy tugged on Satsu's sleeve. After a while, Satsu woke up, turned his head, and saw the silver ship. As soon as he held it in his hand, he began to feel better.

"Mother! Father!" he called. "My pets have brought back my good-luck charm!"

Satsu's parents hurried to his side.

"It's true!" exclaimed his father. "Here is the little silver ship!"

Pressing her hand to Satsu's forehead, his mother cried, "His head is cool. The fever is gone!"

Satsu soon grew strong again. Then his parents invited all their neighbors to a feast. There the fox cub and puppy sat at a table, with Satsu between them. They were served the finest foods and honored as heroes. In a corner, the mouse and his family feasted too. They had been invited by the fox and puppy, who saw to it that they had the tastiest morsels. The animals were fast friends now—a special blessing of the magic silver charm.